They loved shopping, cooking and playing games with their mom.
What they loved most was laying in bed with mom on a
lazy Saturday watching tv and eating cookies.

Kendra and Kara loved spending time with their mom.
It was always the three of them after their father passed away.

Thanks

I want to thank my husband and daughter who allow me the time and space to pursue my passion. I love you both. Special thanks to the many children & families whom I've had the pleasure of working with over the years. I appreciate you for allowing me to walk through the journey with you.

DEDICATION

This book is dedicated to all of the children who deal with the issues stemming from their parents and caregiver's mental illness.

Is Mommy Ok?

Kizzy D. Pittrell

Pam had always been the "cool" mom. She would play games with Kendra and Kara's friends, take them to the park and teach them how to bake.

Every once in awhile, Pam would get very sad. She would lay in the bed for hours and wouldn't play with Kendra or Kara.

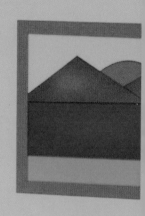

One day Kendra asked if they could watch a movie together, something they always did. Mom yelled at Kendra and slammed her door.

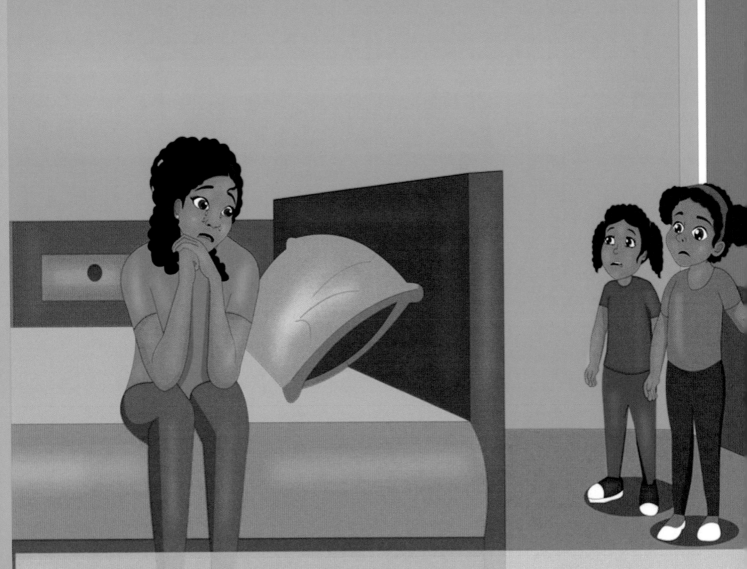

At first the girls thought mom was still sad because she missed daddy. They would see her cry and sometimes she would stay in her bedroom for most of the day.

One day, grandma came to visit. She saw that the house was a mess, the girls had not eaten and mommy was in her room.

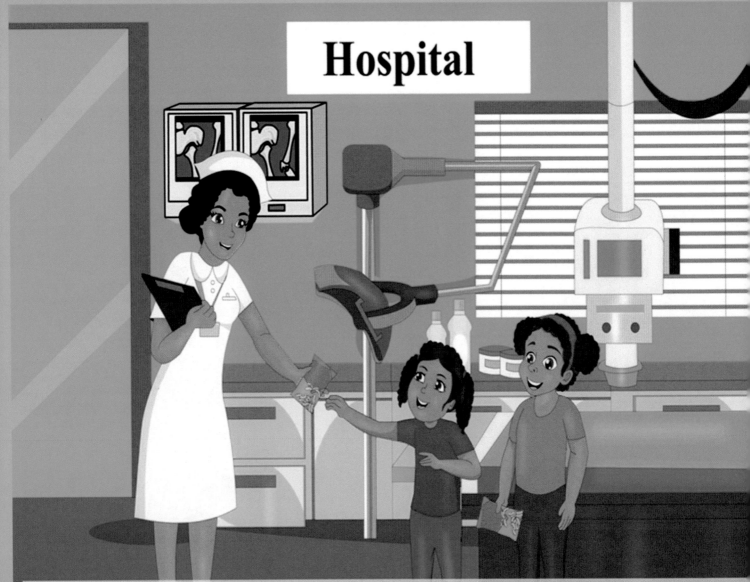

Hospital

Grandma thought mommy wasn't feeling well so she took her to the hospital. Kendra and Kara went along too. At the hospital, the doctors and nurses were very nice. They gave the girls snacks and let them watch a movie while they waited for mommy.

After a while , a nice doctor came out and asked for the family to go in the back to see mommy. Kendra and Kara were so excited to see mommy. They missed making cookies and watching movies together.

The girls heard the doctors tell grandma that mommy had something that begins with the letter "D". But then they heard the doctors tell grandma that mommy has "Depression"!

Depression! What is that and how do you get it? Is this something that mommy can take medicine for? Will mommy be ok? The girls were afraid because they thought that mommy would never get better.

The girls sat down with grandma and the doctor. Dr. Green explained to the girls that depression is normal. The doctor said that depression is when someone feels sad or anxious. He said that all of us will feel sad or anxious sometimes, but people with depression can not always control their feelings. He said that people with depression don't always feel well. Dr. Green asked us did we ever feel sad?

Kara said "yes, I was sad when Carlos told me that I couldn't play basketball with the boys". Dr. Green said yes, depression is the same feeling except people who have it feel sad most of the time, sometimes all day for many days. He also said that people may cry and not want to talk to anyone. He also said people do not always feel well and may need to take medication and talk to someone to feel better.

Kara said, well I never felt like that because Carlos is my friend.
Dr. Green said that our brain helps us to think, act and feel
certain ways. He said that when people are depressed, their
brains work differently than when they are well. Dr. Green said
that depression can be a serious problem but with the help of
you two girls and your grandma, your mom will be ok.

This was great news for Kara and Kendra because now mommy can come home. We will help take care of mommy and she will be ok.

Dr. Green told us that mommy will be coming to see him to talk about how she is feeling. He also said that mommy will have to take medication. Kara asked, "will mommy have to take the same medication like she gives us when we are sick"?

Dr. Green laughed and said "yes, just like your mom has to give you medication to help you feel better, mommy will have to take medication so she can feel better".

Mom was ready to leave the hospital. The girls were so excited to see their mom. Pam gave the girls the biggest hug when she saw Kendra and Kara.

Before we left the hospital, Dr. Green asked us if we had any questions. He said we can always ask him anything we wanted to know about depression. He also told us that we can talk to mommy or grandma about our feelings.

Hospital

We thanked Dr. Green for all of his help. After talking to the doctor we felt better, so did mommy. With lots of talks, hugs and support we know that mommy will be ok.

The End

Recommendations for talking to children about mental illness….

Mental illness can be a challenging topic to explore with children. Many parents do not bring it up for fear that they may not have the words to or are uncomfortable with discussing it. This guide can be used to help parents and caregivers openly talk about mental illness.

1. Tailoring the conversation to the age of the child

There is no age that is too young to start the conversation; however the context of the conversation will be different for a 13 year-old than it would be for a 6 year-old. Make sure that the conversation is appropriate for the developmental age and understanding of the child. One way to discuss this with a young child is to talk about feelings and how everyone feels sad from time to time, but depression is when someone feels sad all of the time.

2. Language

When discussing mental illness with children we want to steer about from language or terms that they may not understand. Language should be clear and tailored to the age of the child; avoiding statistics and terminology that they do not know.

3. Starting the conversation

So where do I start and how? Many parents and caregivers struggle with bringing the topic up. Conversation starters are a great way to have this discussion. Discussing a movie that features a character with a mental illness or a celebrity who has coped with his/her illness is a good conversation starter. Using art, games and books can also aid in discussing mental illness for younger children.

4. Be flexible about how and when a conversation takes place

Be patient, some children may ask questions while playing or may talk more than others. Allow for children to do so because this is how they process information.

5. Do your homework

Have some basic knowledge of mental illness to be able to answer children's questions. It is important to know such things as what is a mental illness, who can get them, what causes them, how are diagnosis made, and what treatments are available.

Made in the USA
Middletown, DE
10 September 2021